outpost zero

CREATED BY **SEAN KELLEY MCKEEVER** & **ALEXANDRE TEFENKGI**

FOR SKYBOUND ENTERTAINMENT ROBERT KIRKMAN Chairman DAVID ALPERT CEO SEAN MACKIEWICZ SVP, Editor-in-Chief SHAWN KIRKHAM SVP, Business Development BRIAN HUNTINGTON VP, Online Content SHAUNA WYNNE Publicity Director ANDRES JUAREZ Art Director JON MOISAN Editor ARIELLE BASICH Associate Editor KATE CAUDILL Assistant Editor CARINA TAYLOR Graphic Designer PAUL SHIN Business Development Manager JOHNNY O'DELL Social Media Manager DAN PETERSEN Sr. Director of Operations & Events Foreign Rights Inquiries ag@sequentialrights.com Other Licensing Inquiries contact@skybound.com WWW.SKYBOUND.COM

IMAGE COMICS, INC. ROBERT KIRKMAN Chief Operating Officer ERIK LARSEN Chief Financial Officer TODD MCFARLANE President MARC SILVESTRI Chief Executive Officer JIM VALENTINO Vice President ERIC STEPHENSON Publisher / Chief Creative Officer JEFF BOISON Director of Publishing Planning & Book Trade Sales CHRIS ROSS Director of Digital Sales JEFF STANG Director of Direct Market Sales KAT SALAZAR Director of PR & Marketing DREW GILL Cover Editor HEATHER DOORNINK Production Manager NICOLE LAPALME Controller WWW.IMAGECOMICS.COM

THE ONLY LIVING THINGS

SEAN KELLEY McKEEVER
CREATOR/WRITER

ALEXANDRE TEFENKGI
CREATOR/ARTIST

JEAN-FRANCOIS BEAULIEU
COLORIST

ARIANA MAHER
LETTERER

ARIELLE BASICH
EDITOR

ANDRES JUAREZ
LOGO DESIGN

CARINA TAYLOR
PRODUCTION DESIGN

OUTPOST ZERO VOLUME 3. FIRST PRINTING. January 2020. Published by Image Comics, Inc. Office of publication: 2701 NW Vaughn St., Ste. 780, Portland, OR 97210. Copyright © 2020 Skybound, LLC. Originally published in single magazine form as OUTPOST ZERO #10-14. OUTPOST ZERO™ (including all prominent characters featured herein), its logo and all character likenesses are trademarks of Skybound, LLC, unless otherwise noted. Image Comics® and its logos are registered trademarks and copyrights of Image Comics, Inc. All rights reserved. No part of this publication may be reproduced or transmitted in any form or by any means (except for short excerpts for review purposes) without the express written permission of Image Comics, Inc. All names, characters, events and locales in this publication are entirely fictional. Any resemblance to actual persons (living or dead), events or places, without satiric intent, is coincidental. Printed in the U.S.A. For information regarding the CPSIA on this printed material call: 203-595-3636.
ISBN: 978-1-5343-1365-1

volume three

SO YOU'RE THINKING...WHAT? WHAT'S THE "IT" SUPPOSED TO BE? THE *BOT*?

LIKE STEVEN SOMEHOW KNEW THERE WAS A BOT DOWN HERE AND, INSTEAD OF SAYING *THAT*, HE GAVE ME SOME CRYPTIC INSTRUCTION?

WELL, IT'S CRYPTIC NO MATTER WHAT, RIGHT?

THAT'S *MY* POINT.

WE SHOULDN'T FOCUS ON WHAT STEVEN SAID, ALEA. WHAT HE DID OR DIDN'T MEAN.

IF WE CAN FIND THE *G.A.P.*....I MEAN, THINK ABOUT ALL THE *ANSWERS* IN THERE.

I KNOW WHAT THIS IS, SAM.

IT'S ABOUT THE GIRL FROM THE RECORDING.

LINDA.

THAT'S NOT...

I MEAN, OF COURSE I'M CURIOUS WHAT ELSE THERE IS OF HER, BUT...

WHATEVER SHE HAD TO SAY...SHE'S GONE. SHE'S BEEN GONE A LONG TIME.

STEVEN BELIEVED WE COULD SAVE EVERYONE FROM DANGER BY COMING DOWN HERE. AS WEIRD A THING AS THAT IS, WE CAN'T *IGNORE* IT.

UM, HI. EXCUSE ME, WE COULD USE SOME HELP...

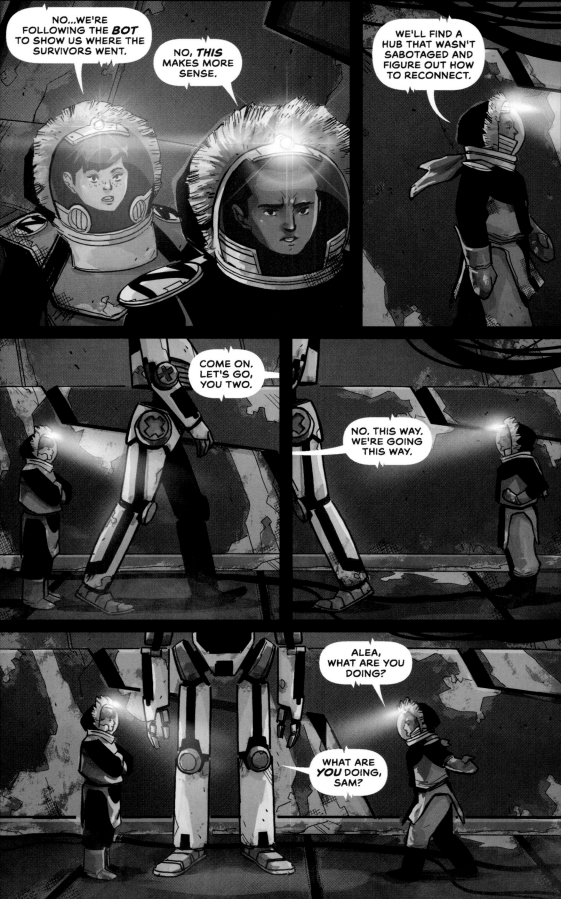

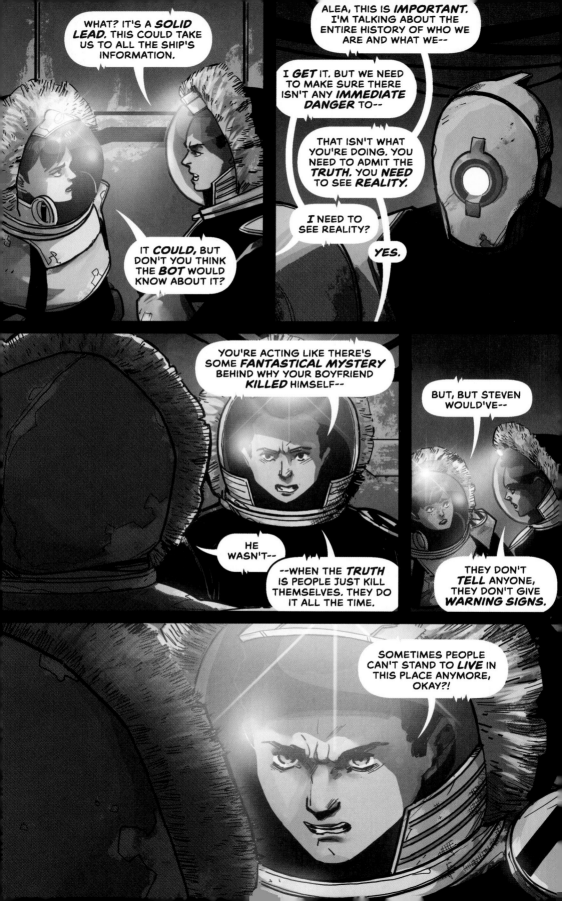

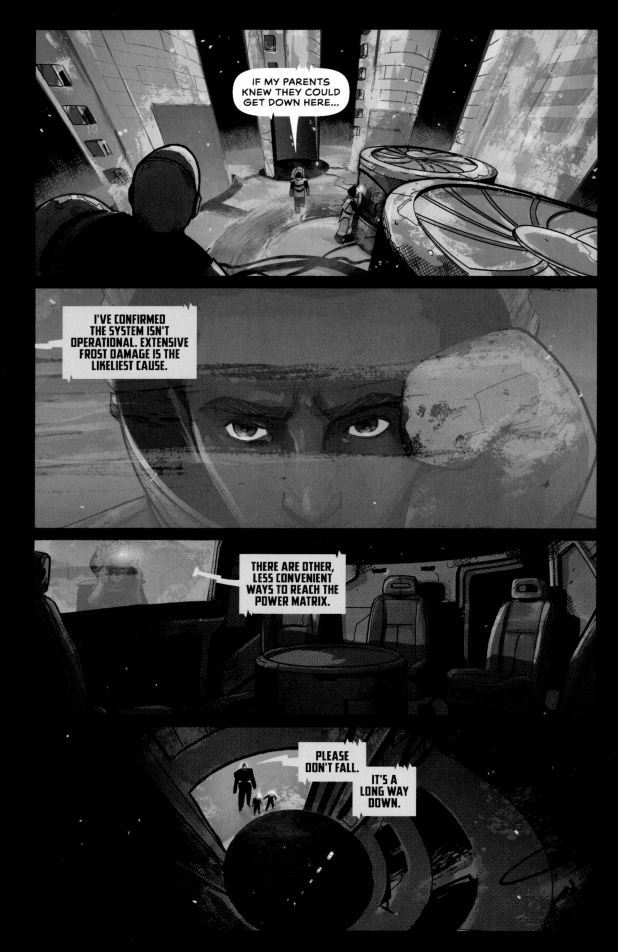

HA HAHA HA!

I SAW HER HAVE BABIES ONCE.

NO, YOU DIDN'T. YOU WOULDA SAID.

IT'S TRUE. SHE HAD *FIVE.* AT THE SAME TIME.

WHOA.

YEAH, MARC SAID SHE HAD BABIES *BEFORE,* TOO. THREE OF THEM.

MARC SAID? IS *NO ONE* TELLING ME STUFF?

I KEEP WONDERING...

LIKE, IF THEY MAKE SO MANY BABIES, AND THOSE BABIES MAKE BABIES...

SHOULDN'T THERE BE WAY *MORE* OF THEM THAN US?

MAYBE IT'S...

MAYBE THEY...

HUH, MAYBE THEY EAT THEIR OWN?

SAM, DO YOU...? WHEN YOU LOOK AT OTHER PEOPLE NOW, DO YOU FEEL THAT?

FEEL WHAT?

LIKE THEY'RE NOT ALL THE WAY ALIVE. LIKE THEY DON'T KNOW *ENOUGH* TO BE.

YOU THOUGHT WE WEREN'T SUPPOSED TO FIND THE G.A.P. BECAUSE PEOPLE DIDN'T WANT US TO.

BUT THE BOT SAID THE NETWORK'S BEEN DOWN SINCE THE CRASH.

SO THE *COMMUNICATIONS SABOTAGE* HAD TO BE A LONG TIME AGO, RIGHT?

I THINK WE'RE THE ONLY ONES WHO KNOW THE G.A.P. *EXISTS.*

AND YOU WANT TO TELL THEM. ABOUT WHAT WE FOUND, ALL OF IT.

SO DO I.

BUT NOT UNTIL WE'VE THOUGHT EVERYTHING *THROUGH.* OKAY?

THIS IS **NOT** OKAY.

WHAT? WE HAVEN'T SAID ANYTHING.

WHENEVER YOU SIT US DOWN LIKE THIS AND STAND IN **FRONT** OF US LIKE THAT, IT MEANS SOMETHING **BAD.**

THE CELL COULD KILL US ALL. LET'S TALK ABOUT WHAT STEVEN DID. THE COUNCIL SHUT DOWN DISCOVERY TEAM.

THOSE'RE JUST THE **RECENT** ONES.

GOOD NEWS, ELLA-- THIS TIME IT'S ACTUALLY **GOOD** NEWS.

GREAT NEWS, IN FACT. AND--

LIFE. WE FOUND **LIFE.**

THE SAMPLING DRILL FROM OUR LAST EXCURSION, I LEFT IT BEHIND WITH THE REST OF OUR CAMP--

BUT DURING THE EMERGENCY I FOUND IT OUTSIDE, NEXT TO THE OUTPOST.

IT WAS THE STORM CELL. THE WINDS BROUGHT THE DRILL *BACK* TO US.

WHAT DOES THAT MEAN? YOU FOUND...

LIKE A CAT, BUT IN THE ICE?

NO, WE FOUND *TRACES* OF SOMETHING THAT LIVED HERE A FEW THOUSAND YEARS AGO.

IT *MEANS* THE FROST SUPPORTED LIFE NOT ALL THAT LONG AGO, AND COULD *AGAIN* SOMEDAY.

IT *COULD* EVEN SUPPORT LIFE RIGHT NOW.

LET'S NOT BE FANTASTICAL. MORE THAN LIKELY IT'S JUST US AND THE CATS.

ALEA? I THOUGHT YOU'D BE MORE EXCITED.

I *AM* EXCITED. IT'S A BIG DEAL, BUT WHAT IF I TOLD YOU...

I FORGOT MY POINT. SORRY.

ARE THE COUNCIL GIVING YOU BACK YOUR JOBS THEN, OR...?

WE HAVEN'T TOLD THE COUNCIL YET.

SHOULDN'T YOU?

IF WE TELL JUST THE COUNCIL, THEY MIGHT NOT WANT THE REST TO KNOW, SO WE'RE ANNOUNCING TO THE WHOLE OUTPOST.

THIS IS TOO BIG AND IMPORTANT TO KEEP IT A SECRET. BUT WE'RE ASKING YOU TO--ONLY FOR NOW.

LIKE I COULD EVEN EXPLAIN IT. I'M GOING TO HEATH'S.

IF EVERYONE FINDS OUT, NO ONE COULD DOWNPLAY WHAT YOU DO ANYMORE.

DISCOVERY TEAM COULD EVEN BE *REINSTATED.*

WE KNOW. THAT'S THE HOPE.

I DON'T KNOW HOW YOU BRING THAT OUT OF HIM.

IT'S JUST BELOW THE SURFACE. YOU HAVE TO KNOW WHAT TO LOOK FOR.

ALTHOUGH THERE WAS SOMETHING ALREADY THERE THIS TIME. HIS NEW FRIENDS, MAYBE.

HE'S BEEN OUT *ALL NIGHT* WITH THEM.

YOU KNOW, HE ADMITS TO *ONE* TRANSGRESSION, SO OF *COURSE* THERE'S ALL THESE THINGS HE'S *NOT* TELLING ME--

KAREN.

SORRY. I'M SORRY. THIS ISN'T HOW YOU WANT TO SPEND YOUR-- I MEAN...

NONSENSE. I'D BE USELESS OTHERWISE. I WAS SIMPLY GOING TO SAY...

IF YOU'RE GOING TO BE *YOURSELF* AND NOT CONFRONT YOUR SON *DIRECTLY*...

THEN BE YOURSELF *ALL* THE WAY. BE THE KAREN WHO WAS MADE SECURITY TEAM CHIEF.

LOOKS LIKE YOU'RE WAITING FOR SOMEONE. PROBABLY NOT ME.

MITCHELL.

LOOK, IF YOU'RE GONNA GET IN MY FACE AGAIN ABOUT--

LYSS TOLD ME.

SHE TOLD ME ALL OF IT. DON'T BE MAD AT HER.

I'M NOT.

YOU ARE.

OKAY, I AM, BUT--

ALEA.

I...YEAH, I KNOW.

BUT NOT WHERE SOMEONE CAN OVERHEAR.

WHATEVER YOU THINK OF ME NOW, I NEED YOU TO HEAR WHAT I HAVE TO SAY.

LYSS CAME TO ME BECAUSE YOU WON'T LISTEN TO--

THAT'S NOT--

LISTEN. YOU NEED TO LISTEN.

I'VE NEVER SEEN HER LIKE THIS, NEITHER HAVE YOU, BARELY SLEEPING, ON EDGE.

SHE'S WORRIED ABOUT YOU.

I KNOW THAT, BUT--

I SAID LISTEN.

SHE THINKS MONSTERS ARE COMING TO SWALLOW EVERYTHING UP. MONSTERS, LIKE IN STORIES.

SHE'S A COMPLETE AND TOTAL WRECK BECAUSE OF YOUR EXPLORATIONS.

IT WAS THE WEIRDEST THING. HE WAS STILL THE SAME MITCHELL, STILL KINDA HOSTILE--

KINDA?

BUT THEN HE WAS... REASONABLE, RATIONAL.

I SAW HIM WITH YOU WHERE WE WERE GONNA MEET. THOUGHT MAYBE IT'D BE A BAD IDEA TO APPROACH. MAYBE NOT, HUH?

I'M GUESSING YOU DIDN'T MENTION WE MIGHT GO *PUBLIC* WITH OUR TRIP INTO THE STEM.

I DIDN'T EVEN *THINK* TO. THE WAY HE WAS BEING, I COULD HARDLY PROCESS IT.

GOING PUBLIC *IS* THE RIGHT THING TO DO. LYSS'LL BE FREE TO *DISCUSS* WHAT HAPPENED.

BUT WHAT LYSS SAW, THAT WAS IN THE *BUNKER*. WE'RE NOT TELLING *ANYONE* THAT PART.

WE SHOULD BE TRANSPARENT, PUT IT *ALL* OUT THERE.

NO, *ABSOLUTELY* NO WAY.

WHY NOT?

WE DON'T KNOW *WHAT* WE SAW DOWN IN THE BUNKER. WE CAN'T--

AND WHAT *BROUGHT* US THERE? WHAT *STEVEN* SAID? AND *HOW* HE GOT INTO THE--

I MEAN--

THIS IS WHAT I MEANT BEFORE, WE HAVEN'T--

LIKE, WHAT ARE THE CONSEQUENCES? WHAT WOULD IT DO TO LYSS? WOULD WE BE BANNED FROM EVER GOING DOWN THERE AGAIN?

HEY.

SAM?

THINK ABOUT WHAT WE SAW, WHAT WE HEARD. WHAT WE *LEARNED.* HOW IT MADE YOU *FEEL.*

WE COULD MAKE *THEM* FEEL THAT WAY.

LOOK AT MITCHELL, HE HARDLY KNOWS ANYTHING AND HE'S *ON OUR SIDE* NOW.

ON *YOUR* SIDE, THAT'S HUGE.

AND LYSS... I MEAN, I DON'T THINK *SHIELDING* HER IS THE SAME AS HELPING HER.

SHE'LL GET PAST THIS, I KNOW IT.

WE DON'T HAVE TO TELL EVERYONE *EVERYTHING.* WHAT STEVEN SAID, THAT WAS FOR US. THE THING IN THE BUNKER CAN WAIT.

KAREN'LL LOSE IT.

BASICALLY THE SAME FOR ME AND MY FOLKS.

"BASICALLY."

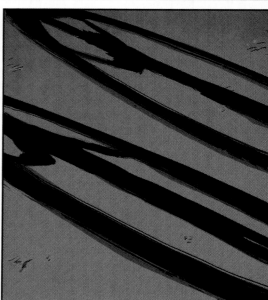

SO WE'RE GONNA DO THIS.

WE'RE GONNA DO THIS...

SHIT.

DON'T GET ME WRONG. THE FIGHTS ARE AMAZING.

IT'S AN INCREDIBLE DISPLAY OF STRENGTH AND COURAGE. I LOVE TO GO.

WHEN MITCHELL STARTED, I STOPPED. THE ARGUMENT WE HAD WAS AN EASY EXCUSE.

TRUTH IS, I'M AFRAID TO WATCH.

WE CAN LEAVE.

AFTER YOUR PARENTS ANNOUNCE, WE DON'T HAVE TO STAY. THERE'S NO REASON TO.

WE COULD GO SEE LYSS.

OR, Y'KNOW, IF YOU WANTED TO GO HOME AND I'D GO HOME AND--Y'KNOW, WHATEVER.

I SHOULD STAY. I SHOULD SUPPORT HIM.

I HEAR HE'S A *FEROCIOUS* FIGHTER. ONE OF THE BEST IN A LONG TIME.

YEAH, ALMOST FOUND THAT OUT A COUPLE TIMES...

SAM...

CHIEF.

VIVIEN, I *TOLD* YOU--

NO, IT'S--

IT'S DOCTOR XI.

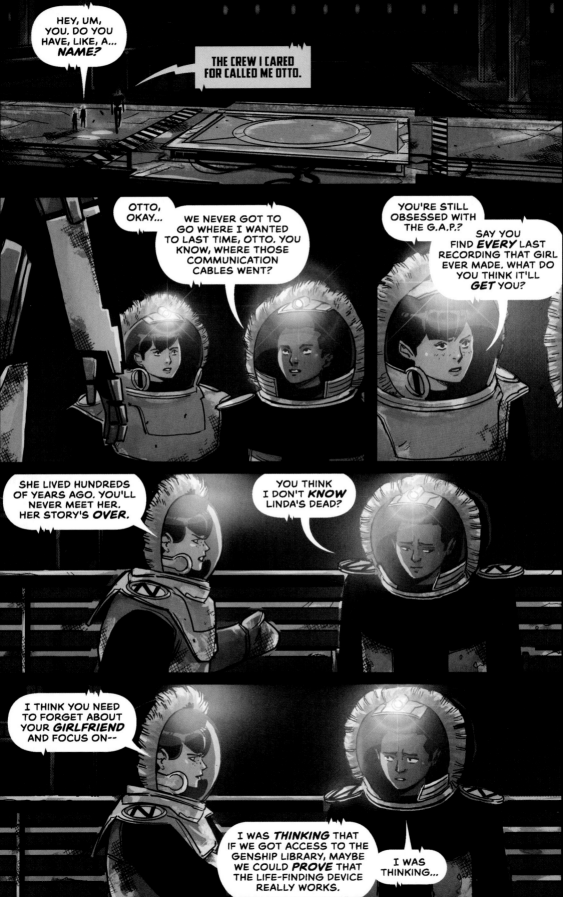

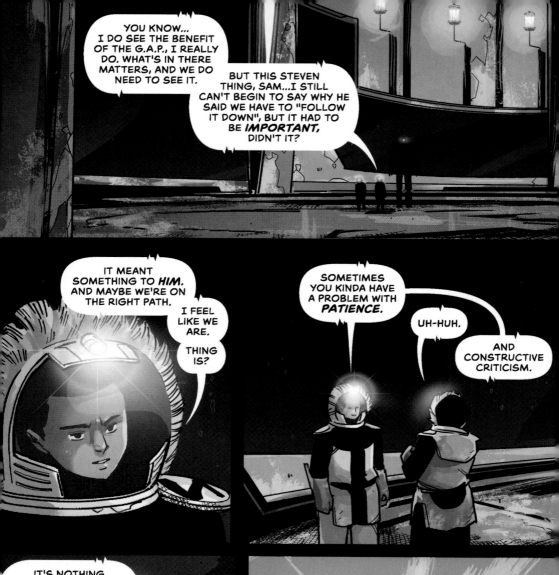

YOU KNOW... I DO SEE THE BENEFIT OF THE G.A.P., I REALLY DO. WHAT'S IN THERE MATTERS, AND WE DO NEED TO SEE IT.

BUT THIS STEVEN THING, SAM...I STILL CAN'T BEGIN TO SAY WHY HE SAID WE HAVE TO "FOLLOW IT DOWN", BUT IT HAD TO BE *IMPORTANT,* DIDN'T IT?

IT MEANT SOMETHING TO *HIM.* AND MAYBE WE'RE ON THE RIGHT PATH.

I FEEL LIKE WE ARE.

THING IS?

SOMETIMES YOU KINDA HAVE A PROBLEM WITH *PATIENCE.*

UH-HUH.

AND CONSTRUCTIVE CRITICISM.

IT'S NOTHING I HAVEN'T HEARD FROM MY MOM, YOU'RE SAYING I NEED TO LEARN TO *WAIT.*

WAIT!

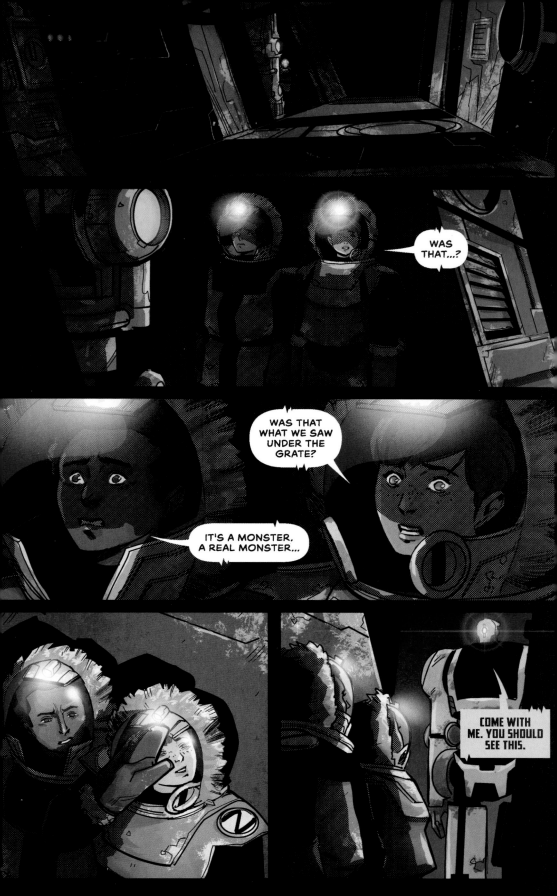

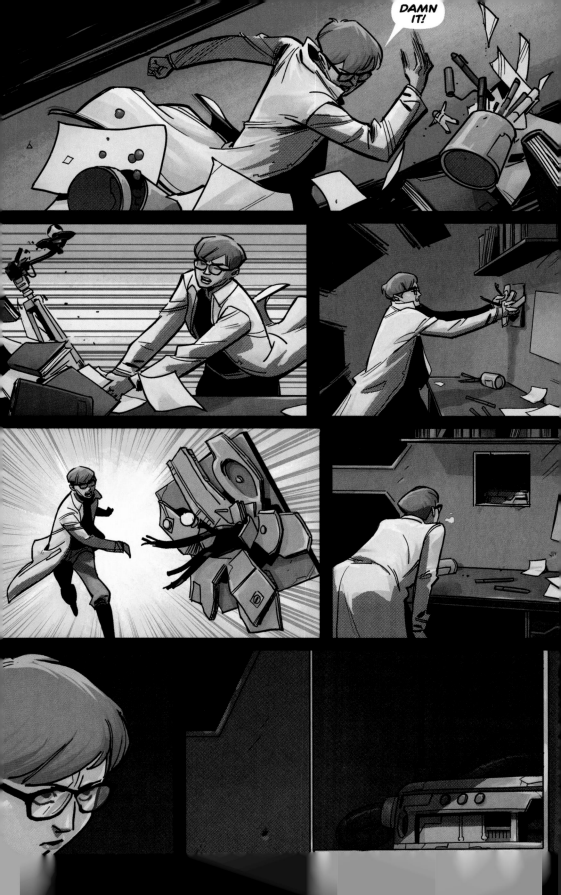

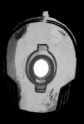

TO DO SO, AS THE BEING EXPLAINS, REQUIRES A PARTICULAR METHOD OF INTERFACE.

IT HAS GIVEN ME INSTRUCTIONS TO TAKE YOU TO AN AIRLOCK, WHERE YOU WILL ENTER THE WATER AND INITIATE CONTACT.

IN THE *WATER?!* THESE AREN'T *SPACE SUITS.* IT'S GOTTA BE BELOW FREEZING, RIGHT? THAT'LL *KILL* US!

YEAH, THAT'S NOT HAPPENING.

THE BEING ASSURES ME IT WILL KEEP YOU SAFE FROM THE PRESSURE AND COLD.

I DON'T GET IT. WHY CAN'T YOU JUST INTERPRET THROUGH THE GLASS?

WHAT THE BEING HAS TO SAY MUST BE SHOWN TO YOU.

I DON'T BUY IT. IT'S *HIDING* SOMETHING.

I'M WITH SAM. THIS DOESN'T SOUND RIGHT.

I HAVE NO INDICATION EITHER WAY. THE BEING DID, HOWEVER, WANT ME TO RELAY TO YOU BOTH...

IT IS SATISFIED THAT YOU HEEDED STEVEN'S MESSAGE.

JANN. OVER HERE.

I KNOW WHAT YOU'RE THINKING.

OH, I BET YOU DON'T, KAREN.

YOU'D LOVE TO GO *EXPLORING* DOWN HERE. YOU'RE THINKING WE COULD PUT A *HATCH* OVER THAT HOLE INSTEAD OF A SUBSTANTIAL LAYER OF *NEW FLOORING.*

YOU CAN *FORGET* IT.

I CAN'T UNSEE *ANY* OF THIS. YOU SHOULD'VE CONSIDERED THAT BEFORE COMING TO ME.

I DID, BUT YOU HAVE TO BE DOWN HERE *WITH* ME.

WHY'S THAT?

KAREN...?

MY SON, YOUR DAUGHTER.

OUR RESPONSIBILITY.

> RECORD HOLOVID
> GENSHIP ANCESTRY PROJECT
> AUDVID CALIBRATION

SAM, DID THE BEING TELL YOU OF THIS PLACE? HOW CAN IT KNOW?

G.A.P. RECORD SEARCH
BY NAME: LINDA-
MATCHING: 1,202,662

SAM?

OTTO. GIVE ME A MINUTE TO--

AH, RIGHT.

G.A.P. RECORD SEARCH
BY RECORDING NUMBER: 619-
MATCHING: ...

GOT IT.

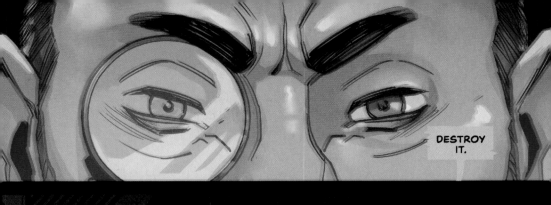

DESTROY IT.

I DON'T-- I CAN'T-- I...

DID *YOU KNOW* ANY OF THIS?

THIS IS ENTIRELY NEW INFORMATION.

EVEN WHY GENSHIP OH-EIGHT *CRASHED?*

I WASN'T AWARE OF THESE DETAILS, SAM.

YOU SAID ONCE YOU CAN'T CHANGE YOUR DESIGN, BUT YOU CAN CHANGE YOUR PURPOSE.

YES, THAT'S TRUE.

OKAY. SO...

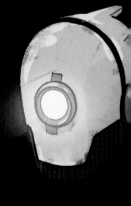

WHAT ABOUT ME? CAN *I* CHANGE YOUR PURPOSE?

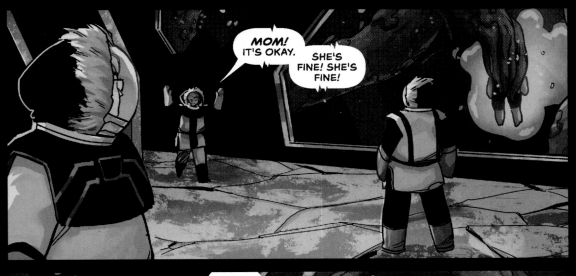

the end

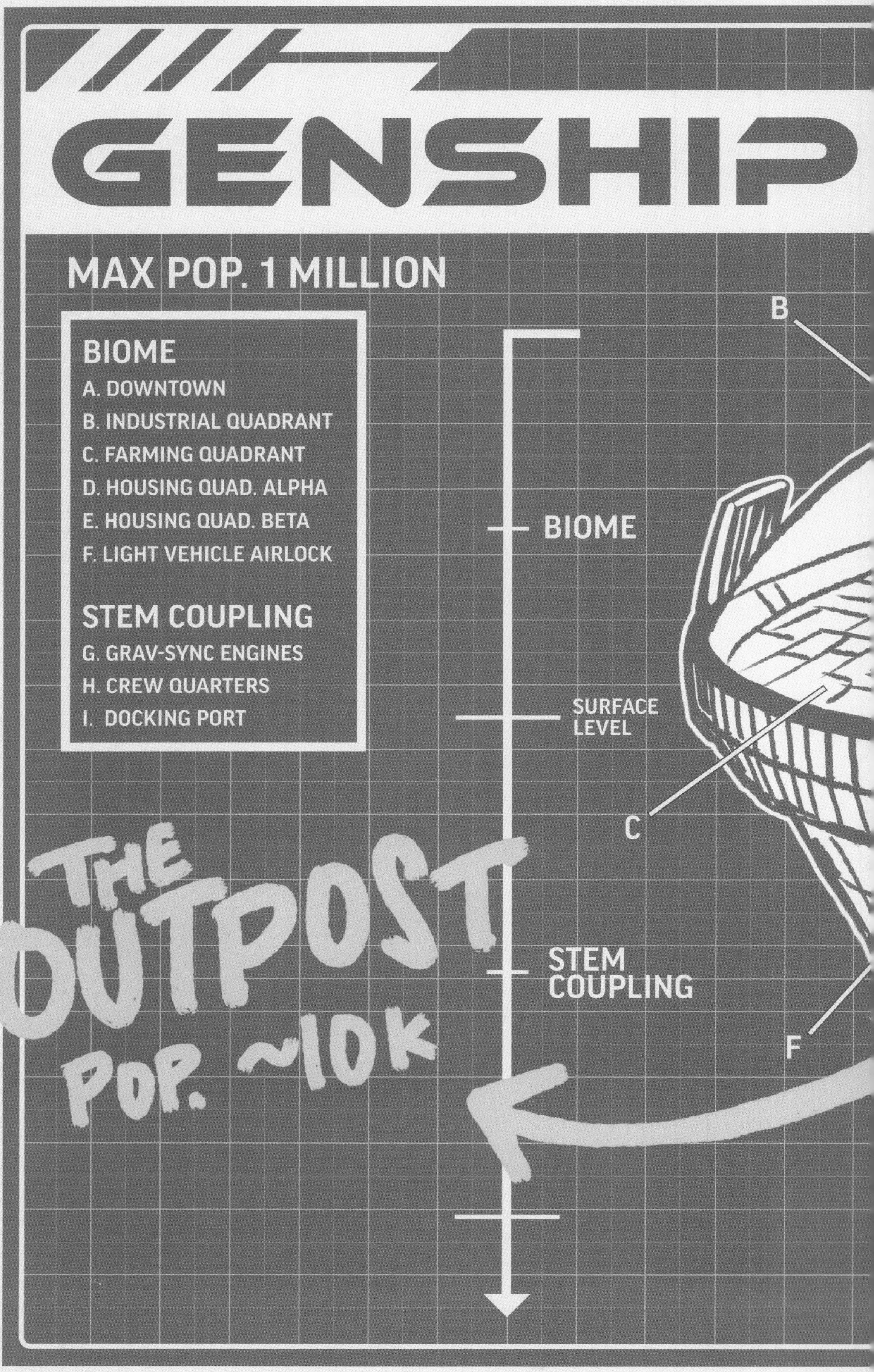

GENSHIP

MAX POP. 1 MILLION

BIOME
A. DOWNTOWN
B. INDUSTRIAL QUADRANT
C. FARMING QUADRANT
D. HOUSING QUAD. ALPHA
E. HOUSING QUAD. BETA
F. LIGHT VEHICLE AIRLOCK

STEM COUPLING
G. GRAV-SYNC ENGINES
H. CREW QUARTERS
I. DOCKING PORT

BIOME

SURFACE
LEVEL

STEM
COUPLING

B

C

F

THE OUTPOST
POP. ~10K

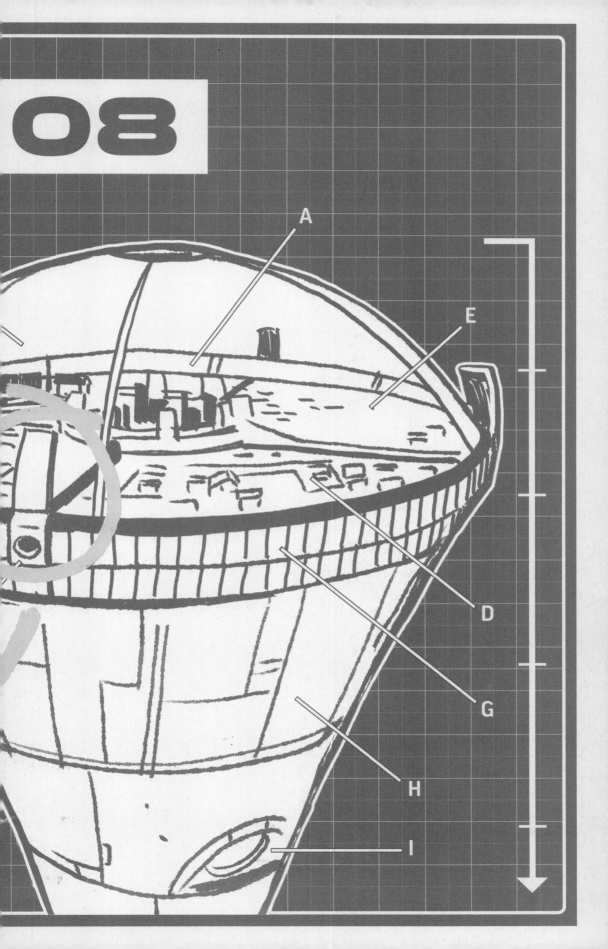

08

A

E

D

G

H

I

For more tales from ROBERT KIRKMAN and SKYBOUND

MURDER FALCON TP
ISBN: 978-1-5343-1235-7
$19.99

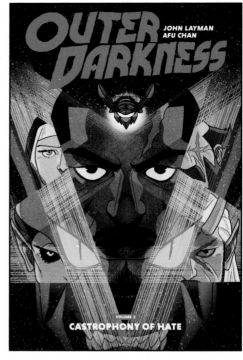

VOL. 1: EACH OTHER'S THROATS
ISBN: 978-1-5343-1210-4
$16.99

VOL. 2: CASTROPHANY OF HATE
ISBN: 978-1-5343-1370-5
$16.99

VOL. 1: HOMECOMING TP
ISBN: 978-1-63215-231-2
$9.99

VOL. 2: CALL TO ADVENTURE TP
ISBN: 978-1-63215-446-0
$12.99

VOL. 3: ALLIES AND ENEMIES TP
ISBN: 978-1-63215-683-9
$12.99

VOL. 4: FAMILY HISTORY TP
ISBN: 978-1-63215-871-0
$12.99

VOL. 5: BELLY OF THE BEAST TP
ISBN: 978-1-5343-0218-1
$12.99

VOL. 6: FATHERHOOD TP
ISBN: 978-1-53430-498-7
$14.99

VOL. 7: BLOOD BROTHERS TP
ISBN: 978-1-5343-1053-7
$14.99

VOL. 8: LIVE BY THE SWORD TP
ISBN: 978-1-5343-1368-2
$14.99

VOL. 1: DEEP IN THE HEART TP
ISBN: 978-1-5343-0331-7
$16.99

VOL. 2: THE EYES UPON YOU TP
ISBN: 978-1-5343-0665-3
$16.99

VOL. 3: LONGHORNS TP
ISBN: 978-1-5343-1050-6
$16.99

VOL. 4: LONE STAR TP
ISBN: 978-1-5343-1367-5
$16.99

CHAPTER ONE
ISBN: 978-1-5343-0642-4
$9.99

CHAPTER TWO
ISBN: 978-1-5343-1057-5
$16.99

CHAPTER THREE
ISBN: 978-1-5343-1326-2
$16.99

VOL. 1
ISBN: 978-1-60706-420-6
$9.99

VOL. 2
ISBN: 978-1-60706-568-5
$14.99

VOL. 3
ISBN: 978-1-60706-667-5
$12.99

VOL. 4
ISBN: 978-1-60706-843-3
$12.99